← You Ch[oose]

SCOOBY-DOO!

THE CASE OF THE
CLOWN
CARNIVAL

STONE ARCH BOOKS
a capstone imprint

You Choose Stories: Scooby-Doo
is published by Stone Arch Books,
A Capstone Imprint
1710 Roe Crest Drive
North Mankato, Minnesota 56003
www.mycapstone.com

Copyright © 2017 Hanna-Barbera.
SCOOBY-DOO and all related characters and elements
are trademarks of © Hanna-Barbera and
WB SHIELD: ™ & © Warner Bros. Entertainment Inc.
(s17)

CAPS37489

All rights reserved. No part of this publication may be
reproduced in whole or in part, or stored in a retrieval
system, or transmitted in any form or by any means,
electronic, mechanical, photocopying, recording, or
otherwise, without written permission of the publisher.

Cataloging-in-Publication Data is available on the
Library of Congress website.
ISBN: 978-1-4965-4333-2 [Library Hardcover]
ISBN: 978-1-4965-4335-6 [Paperback]
ISBN: 978-1-4965-4337-0 [eBook PDF]
978-1-4965-5388-1 [Reflowable epub]

Summary: It's a Scooby-Doo reunion when Scooby and
the rest of the Mystery Inc. gang gather at a circus
carnival under the big top. But when the clowns enter
the ring, things go from merry to mayhem — the
clowns turn into robots!

Printed in Canada.
10050S17

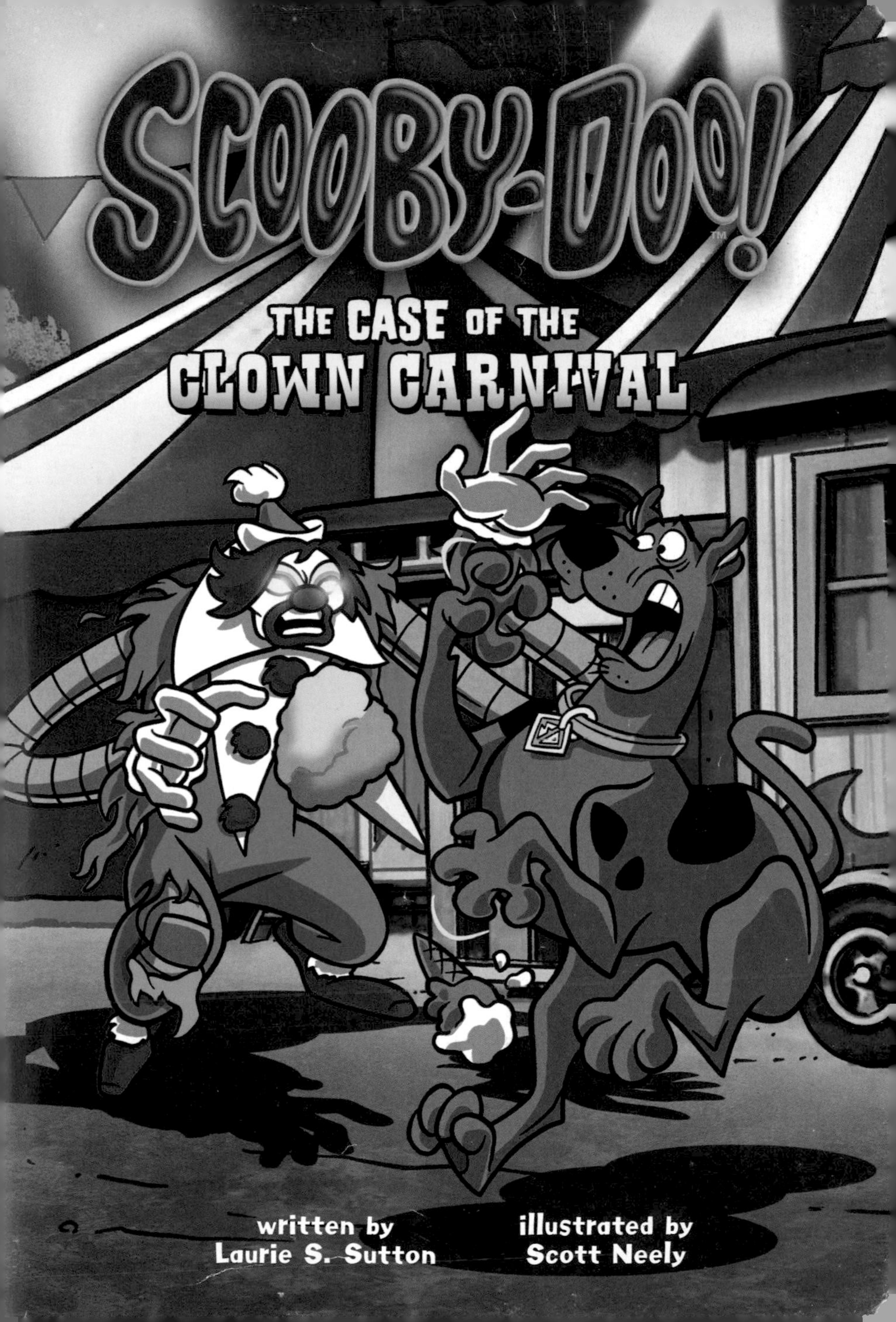
SCOOBY-DOO!™
THE CASE OF THE
CLOWN CARNIVAL
written by
Laurie S. Sutton
illustrated by
Scott Neely

THE MYSTERY INC. GANG!

SCOOBY-DOO

SKILLS: Loyal; super snout
BIO: This happy-go-lucky hound avoids scary situations at all costs, but he'll do anything for a Scooby Snack!

SHAGGY ROGERS

SKILLS: Lucky; healthy appetite
BIO: This laid-back dude would rather look for grub than search for clues, but he usually finds both!

FRED JONES JR.

SKILLS: Athletic; charming
BIO: The leader and oldest member of the gang. He's a good sport — and good at them, too!

DAPHNE BLAKE

SKILLS: Brains; beauty
BIO: As a sixteen-year-old fashion queen, Daphne solves her mysteries in style.

VELMA DINKLEY

SKILLS: Clever; highly intelligent
BIO: Although she's the youngest member of Mystery Inc., Velma's an old pro at catching crooks.

A family reunion at the circus takes a turn for the worse when the clowns are revealed to be robots with sinister plans. But who — or what — is behind this big top brainteaser? Only **YOU** can help Scooby-Doo and the rest of the Mystery Inc. gang track down the clown culprits.

Follow the directions at the bottom of each page. The choices **YOU** make will change the outcome of the story. After you finish one path, go back and read the others for more Scooby-Doo adventures!

YOU CHOOSE the path to solve . . .

THE CASE OF THE CLOWN CARNIVAL

Scooby-Doo sticks his head out of the window of the Mystery Machine as it drives down the road. He sniffs the air. The smells that come to his nose make his eyes pop wide and his mouth drool.

"Ri smell rot dogs!" Scooby says.

Scooby's best pal, Shaggy, pokes his head out of the window too. He inhales the aromas of the cooking hot dogs and drools almost as much as Scooby. The driver in the car behind them has to use the windshield wipers to swish away their excessive saliva.

"Like, we're almost there, Scoobs!" Shaggy exclaims. "Circus food, here we come!"

"Don't you mean, family reunion, here we come?" asks Daphne Blake, another member of Mystery Inc. "We're here to see our relatives, after all."

Turn the page.

"I can't wait to see my parents and my sister, Madelyn," Velma says.

"My folks are coming too," Daphne adds. "Dad might buy the circus to add to the zoo on our estate."

"Are your sisters coming?" Fred asks hopefully.

Velma nudges Daphne. "He means, is your sister, Dawn, the fashion model, coming," she says. "I think he has a crush on her."

"Like, why would he have a crush on Dawn and not Daphne? All of the sisters look identical," Shaggy blurts.

Fred hits a bump in the road to distract them, and Shaggy and Scooby are tossed to the back of the van. There they find a box of Scooby Snacks. In seconds, they forget all about what Shaggy said.

A few minutes later, the Mystery Machine pulls into the parking lot. The big top is just up ahead. The gang sees their families waving hello.

"Scoobert! How's my little pup?" Mama-Doo asks Scooby as he bounces out of the van.

"Raww, Mom!" Scooby moans, embarrassed.

"Norville! There's my boy!" Shaggy's mother says.

"Aww, Mom!" Shaggy sighs and rolls his eyes, embarrassed when his mom uses his real name too.

"Hiya, nephew! Solved any good mysteries lately?" Shaggy's uncle asks, shaking his hand.

ZZZAAAPPP! A joy buzzer zings Shaggy's palm.

"Zoinks! Uh, hi, Uncle Gaggy," Shaggy replies.

"That trick never gets old," Gaggy says, laughing.

A large dog wearing a clown hat and fluffy collar holds his paw out for Scooby to shake. "Hi, Rooby."

"Ruh, hi, Cousin Whoopsy," Scooby replies. He looks suspiciously at his cousin's paw. Suddenly a jet of water squirts from a fake flower on Whoopsy's collar and splashes Scooby in the face.

Daphne's dad laughs. "Those two are such practical jokers!" he says. "I'm glad they're here to help me decide if I want to buy the circus."

Just then a man in a ringmaster's suit and top hat appears. "Welcome to the Badumdum Circus and Carnival! I'm Bo Badumdum, the owner," he greets them.

Turn the page.

Clowns dressed in colorful costumes dance and leap around the circus owner to entertain the special guests.

"Come with me to the big top! I've arranged an exclusive performance for you!" Bo says.

As everyone enters the giant tent, Velma nudges her sister, Madelyn. "Did those clowns look odd to you?" she asks.

"No." Madelyn shrugs. "It was just like when I was in clown school. Why?"

The Mystery Inc. gang and their families take their seats in a special section and wait for the show to begin. Scooby and Shaggy load up on cotton candy, popcorn, and peanuts.

SCARRRF! SCARRRF! The food disappears

"**BUUUURP!** Like, now what, Scoob?" Shaggy moans, sad to see all their snacks are gone.

Scooby pulls out a box of Scooby Snacks. "Ri brought backup."

The ringmaster steps to the center of the big top. "*Laaaadies* and *gennnntlemen*! Presenting the world-famous Bwaha Clowns!"

A dozen costumed characters run out into the center ring. They ride miniature unicycles and throw buckets of confetti at each other. The crowd laughs at the harmless fun.

But suddenly it's not so harmless. One of the clowns' arms turns into a metallic rope. It grabs Daphne's father and pulls him from his seat!

The head of another clown flies off like a rocket and hits the center tent pole. **CRAAACK!** The pole splits, and the tent canvas starts to collapse!

Scooby and Shaggy gobble down Scooby Snacks for comfort. But then . . . **SNAAATCH!** A metallic clown hand swipes the Scooby Snacks!

"I *knew* something was wrong with those clowns!" Velma declares. "They're robots!"

"They've kidnapped my dad!" Daphne yells. "I'm going after him!"

"They're bringing down the big top!" Fred shouts. "Velma, help me stop it!"

"They stole our Scooby Snacks! Scooby-Doo, what are we going to do?" Shaggy moans.

To follow Scooby and Shaggy, turn to page 12.

To follow Fred and Velma, turn to page 14.

To follow Daphne, turn to page 16.

The mechanical clown pedals away on a miniature unicycle. Its legs spin like pinwheels in the wind, but the bike still doesn't go very fast.

The clown juggles the Scooby Snacks above its head. "Hahahaha!" it laughs in an artificial voice.

"Hey! Scooby Snacks are not toys!" Shaggy yells as he watches his treat spin in the air.

The clown circles the ring and careens toward the exit. The robot head twists around to look at Shaggy and Scooby. Then it sticks its stainless steel tongue out at the two pals. *PHHHHFFFFT!*

"Like, that's our last box," Shaggy realizes. "We've got to get it back!"

"Scooby-Dooby-Doo!" Scooby declares, trying to sound brave. He takes off after the clown.

"Oh, man, the things I do for Scooby Snacks!" Shaggy says as he takes off after Scooby.

Unfortunately Shaggy doesn't get very far. He trips on a pair of giant clown shoes and goes flying through the air. He lands on a mini trampoline and bounces even higher.

Scooby watches as Shaggy shoots up into the air and bursts through the canvas of the big top.

"Hahahaha!" the robot clown laughs as it pedals past Scooby and escapes out the tent flap.

Scooby gallops out of the big top and finds Shaggy's dad and Uncle Gaggy.

"Scooby-Doo! We've got to catch that criminal clown!" Shaggy's dad says.

"It's not a criminal. It's a new clown act!" Gaggy protests.

"B-but, rut about Raggy?!" Scooby whimpers.

"Look! There's a trail of footprints. Maybe Shaggy is following the robot that direction," Mr. Rogers says.

"But look over there! There's a trail of snack crumbs. Maybe Shaggy is eating the Scooby Snacks while he's chasing the robot in the other direction," Gaggy replies.

"Rhich ray do ri go?" Scooby wonders.

If Scooby follows the footprints, turn to page 18.
If Scooby follows the snack crumbs, turn to page 25.

The robot clown's head hits the main tent pole like a cannonball. **SMAAAASH!** The wood splits and splinters. The massive tent starts to fall. The audience screams and runs in every direction except toward the exits!

"Come on, Velma! I've got a plan!" Fred announces.

He grabs Velma by the hand and runs toward a hot air balloon in the center ring. A big sign hanging on the basket reads *FREE RIDES*!

"This isn't time for fun, Fred!" Velma protests.

"Nope. This is all business," Fred says as they jump in. "We can use the balloon to support the tent canvas until everyone can escape."

"That . . . that's brilliant, Fred. I'm impressed," Velma replies. But she changes her mind when she sees Fred fumble with the controls.

"Do you know how to drive one of these things?" Velma asks.

"Sure! I can drive anything!" Fred replies confidently. "Now where's the ignition switch?"

Velma points at a giant red button.

"I knew that," Fred says.

FWOOOOOSH! A burst of flame leaps out of the burner and into the center of the balloon. The air heats up and lifts the balloon off the ground.

"Mystery Inc. to the rescue!" Fred declares as the balloon floats toward the top of the tent.

CRAAACK! SNAAAAP! The main pole splits in two. The canvas starts to collapse. The tent falls straight toward Fred and Velma — and their fragile balloon!

FLOPPP! The circus tent safely drapes over the balloon. Fred keeps the big top aloft long enough for the crowd to escape.

"Um, how do *we* get out of here?" Velma asks.

"We can use this sharp grappling hook to cut through the tent," Fred suggests. "Or we can slide down the mooring rope. Which one do you think is best?"

If Fred and Velma use the grappling hook, turn to page 21.
If Fred and Velma slide down the rope, turn to page 27.

Daphne's father struggles in the grip of the robot clown. The clown's feet suddenly transform into wheels and it speeds across the center ring.

HONK! HONK! The robot squeezes its red nose to warn the other clowns to get out of the way.

"Quick! We have to stop that mechanical monster before it gets away with Dad!" Daphne yells. She leaps out of her seat and jumps into the circus ring.

"Wait for me!" her four identical sisters all say at the same time. They take off after Daphne.

The Blake sisters chase the fleeing robot, but the real clowns accidentally get in the way. A super-long trick scarf springs from one of their pockets and wraps around Daphne's ankle. She trips and falls, and her sisters fall on top of her, one after the other.

THWUMP! THWUMP! THWUMP! They pile up like a stack of pancakes.

Daphne watches the mechanical kidnapper zoom out of the tent with her father.

"Re robot's retting aray," Daphne struggles to say with her face squashed under her siblings.

The real clowns shove a circus teeter-totter board under the sisters and lift up one end with a toy car jack. They pump and pump until the Blake sisters are upright and can separate.

"I'm taking command of this rescue mission!" Daphne's sister, Delilah, announces. "I have the military skills and training for search and rescue."

"Yeah. Delilah's the Marine Corps officer, Daph. You're an amateur compared to her," Dorothy Blake agrees.

"Hey, Daphne's smart enough for Mystery Inc.," Dawn Blake points out.

"Says the fashion model," Delilah smirks.

"Aaaand sibling rivalry strikes again," Daisy Blake observes.

"And, while we've been standing here arguing, the robot clown is getting away!" Daphne states. "Listen, Delilah, I have my skill set, and you have yours. Let's split up. It's a Mystery Inc. tradition."

To follow Delilah, turn to page 23.
To follow Daphne, turn to page 29.

Scooby decides to follow the footprints. Shaggy's dad goes along with him.

"This reminds me of when I was a police officer. Following a lead and chasing down bad guys; those were the good old days," Mr. Rogers says.

The trail leads toward the circus midway, which is lined with game kiosks and food stalls. Scooby's nose sniffs the delicious aromas, and his tummy rumbles. His mouth begins to drool.

"Don't lose your focus," Mr. Rogers warns.

"Right!" Scooby replies and turns his attention back to the trail of footprints.

Suddenly, they hear a faint wail: "Scooby-Doooo! Where are yoooou?"

"Raggy!" Scooby exclaims. He takes off running.

"Scooby! Wait! We're supposed to be following the trail!" Mr. Rogers shouts after the galloping canine. But it's no use.

"Ri'm coming, Raggy!" Scooby howls as he leaves Shaggy's dad behind.

Scooby finds his friend sitting on top of a giant plastic ice cream cone at the center of a kiddie ride with twirling swings. The kids are laughing, but the ride operator is shaking his fist at Shaggy.

"Hey! Get down from there! You're too old for this ride!" the guy yells.

"Like, I can't! I'm stuck!" Shaggy hollers.

Scooby pushes the *OFF* button with his paw. The ride slows and comes to a stop.

"Awww!" the kids grumble. They climb out of the seats. But Shaggy is still stuck on the top of the ride.

"I'll think of a ray to rave you," Scooby promises.

"Um, think fast, Scoob!" Shaggy says and points to the robot clown rushing toward them.

"Ruh-roh!" Scooby exclaims.

The clown grabs one of the hanging swings and uses it to spin the ride around and around until Shaggy gets tossed from the top.

Shaggy flies through the air — again!

If Shaggy lands on the high-speed roller-coaster, turn to page 32.
If Shaggy lands in a giant fish tank, turn to page 48.

"I think the grappling hook is the fastest way out of here," Velma decides.

"Good call," Fred agrees. He grabs the heavy hook and uses it to slice through the tent canvas. *RIIIIIP!*

Fred and Velma climb out of the basket and through the hole just as the balloon starts to deflate. Everything begins to sink. The high, pointed tip of the big top dips down to form a crater that pulls Fred and Velma back toward the tent's hole.

"Jinkies!" Velma gasps.

"Hang on, Velma!" Fred warns.

Their weight carries them back down through the hole. Fred and Velma grab the edge of the torn canvas, and the fabric rips into a giant ribbon. They ride it like a zip line all the way to the ground.

The pair hits the center ring and tumbles over each other. Velma's glasses go flying off her face.

"My glasses! I can't see anything without my glasses!" Velma exclaims.

Turn the page.

Fred looks up and sees the balloon and the big top falling toward them. "Maybe it's better that you can't see anything right now," he says.

Fred pulls Velma to her feet, and they run for the exit. Along the way he sees her glasses and grabs them off the ground.

The pair barely makes it out of the big top in time. **FWOOOMP!** The giant tent collapses! The force knocks them off their feet. Fred loses hold of Velma's glasses, which soar out of sight.

"Velma! Fred! Are you okay?" Madelyn Dinkley exclaims as she runs up to her sister. "Um, Velma, where are your glasses?"

"I had them, but I lost them," Fred says. "Sorry, Velma."

"We'll find them, sis," Madelyn promises, taking her sister's arm and guiding her away.

As soon as the girls leave, a voice whispers to Fred from the shadows: "Follow me if you want to solve this mystery!"

To follow Velma, turn to page 34.
To follow Fred, turn to page 52.

Delilah Blake marches away from her sisters. She doesn't look back to see if anyone follows.

"The Corps can stand alone!" Delilah declares.

She stomps out of the big top and finds Fred's uncle. Karl Jones is using all his strength to hold a set of 200-pound barbells above his head.

"Come with me, strongman. I'm recruiting you!" Delilah says.

"Oh, hi, Delilah," Karl replies as he swings the weights safely to the ground. "What's up?"

"George Blake has been abducted by a robot clown of unknown allegiance. It is presumed to be hostile," Delilah replies.

"Your dad's been kidnapped?" Karl gasps. "What are we waiting for? Let's go find him!"

"Follow me," Delilah orders.

As they move out, a young voice calls to them: "Wait for me! I want to help!" Skippy-Doo says.

The small pup scampers up to Delilah and Karl. He wears glasses and an enthusiastic grin.

Turn the page.

24

"What's your skill set, recruit?" Delilah asks.

"I'm good at solving mysteries," Skippy replies.

"You've got a good pedigree," Delilah admits. "Fall in."

Skippy-Doo jumps into line next to Uncle Karl.

"Forward, march!" Delilah orders. She leads her army of two toward the carnival midway.

"Look! A clue!" Skippy says almost immediately.

"Eyes forward, recruit!" Delilah snaps.

"But —" Skippy protests.

"I'm in charge here," Delilah reminds the pup.

Skippy follows his leader, but the clue he saw sticks in his mind. The farther away from it he gets, the more it bothers him. Suddenly he turns runs back the way he came.

"Deserter!" Delilah declares. "I'll have you court-martialed!"

"That's okay. You've still got my muscles," Karl proclaims and flexes his biceps. "Let's keep going."

To follow Skippy-Doo, turn to page 36.
To follow Delilah and Karl, turn to page 55.

Scooby decides to follow the trail of crumbs. Shaggy's Uncle Gaggy jogs alongside Scooby.

"Whoopsy-Doo, where are you?" Gaggy calls out for his canine companion.

Scooby's cousin, Whoopsy, leaps out from behind a small tent as if to scare them. But his goofy grin and hat are too funny to be frightening. Gaggy laughs at Whoopsy's antics. Scooby concentrates on finding Shaggy and pays no attention.

"Scooby-Doo, when did you lose your sense of humor?" Gaggy says.

"Rit's not rost. Raggy is rost, and Ri have to rind him," Scooby replies.

"Now rat's a real friend!" Whoopsy sobs dramatically and hugs Gaggy. Both of them pull out giant handkerchiefs and pretend to blow their noses. Confetti shoots out of the handkerchiefs.

Scooby follows the trail of snack crumbs. It leads him through the crowds of happy families enjoying a day at the circus and carnival. But all the different scents start to interfere with Scooby's nose.

Turn the page.

Suddenly the trail ends. There are no more crumbs to follow. Scooby sniffs the air, but all he can smell is cotton candy and corn dogs. This would be a good thing, except that now Scooby can't track Shaggy!

Scooby stops in his tracks. "Ruh-roh," he says.

Scooby starts to imagine being without Shaggy forever. Then he starts to sob. "Boo hoo hoo! Ri'll never see my best friend again!"

Scooby's nose gets all blocked up. Now it's really impossible to sniff out Shaggy. Gaggy and Whoopsy offer Scooby their handkerchiefs. More confetti shoots out, and Scooby wails louder.

Scooby's distress attracts a crowd. They want to help. When they find out that the dog has lost his human, they all volunteer to join in the search.

"This way!" a man says.

"No, this way!" a woman insists.

Scooby can't go in both directions. He has to choose one!

If Scooby goes along with the man, turn to page 68.
If Scooby goes along with the woman, turn to page 86.

"The quickest way out of here is to slide down the rope," Velma decides.

Fred and Velma hop out of the basket and grip the mooring rope. It's smooth, and they climb down down the line easily. They are near the ground when Velma suddenly stops. Fred bumps into her and almost knocks both of them off the rope.

"Uh-oh. It looks like we have a welcoming committee," Velma says. Below her one of the robot clowns is waiting. Its eyes glow a fearsome red.

"Quick! Get back to the balloon," Fred says.

The robot sees them climbing up the rope. It grabs the mooring line and tries to shake Fred and Velma off. They barely make it back into the basket.

"Well, I guess we have to use the grappling hook after all," Velma says with a shrug.

Fred hacks at the tent canvas with the sharp points of the hook.

"Hurry, Fred! The clown is climbing the rope!" Velma hollers.

Turn the page.

Fred slices as fast as he can. Velma pulls at the hole in the tent to help widen the opening. But as she's pulling, she accidentally hits the balloon's burner button.

FWHOOOOOOSH! The flame leaps high into the balloon. The balloon starts to rise.

RIIIIIP! The weakened tent canvas splits wide open, and the hot air balloon slips through the gap. The big top collapses behind them.

"Uh-oh, we've got a passenger," Velma says. She points at the robot clown, still clinging halfway up the mooring line.

"We've also got backup," Fred announces as he sees the rest of Mystery Inc. on the ground below. "Hi, guys! We could use some help!"

Scooby-Doo chomps onto the end of the mooring line with his teeth. Shaggy and Daphne grab the rope and dig in their heels. The balloon slows, but the drag from the rope causes it to turn toward the whirling Ferris wheel.

If the balloon hits the ride, turn to page 71.
If the balloon misses the ride, turn to page 89.

Daphne follows the robot clown out of the big top. It has a head start, but it's easy to tell which way it went. Crowds of people are shrieking and running away from the wild machine. Daphne starts to run into the chaos.

"You need to be faster than that," Dorothy declares as she drives past Daphne in a small clown car.

"She always wants to win the race," Daphne mutters as her sister, the racecar driver, speeds away. Then she spots something that makes her smile — a mini motorcycle parked near the big top.

Daphne hops onto the miniature motorbike and grips the tiny handlebars. She twists the throttle, and the vehicle peels out.

BEEP! BEEP! The horn squeaks as Daphne warns people to get out of the way. She swerves through the crowd and catches up to Dorothy.

Dorothy looks surprised when Daphne pulls up alongside the clown car, but then she smiles and speeds up. The siblings zoom down the deserted midway. They can see the robot clown at the end.

Turn the page.

Suddenly the robot's clown shoes expand in size, and its legs extend. It's a giant! The mechanical menace rises up into the air and stomps toward the sisters.

"Jeepers," Daphne gulps.

Daphne and Dorothy avoid the lumbering giant and drive up the slope of a roller-coaster loop. They spin around and around on the track as the robot tries to grab them.

"This is crazy!" Dorothy shouts.

"This is normal — for Mystery Inc.!" Daphne replies.

"What would Mystery Inc. do in this situation?" Dorothy asks.

"Split up!" Daphne yells. She jumps the mini cycle off the track. Dorothy drives the clown car in the opposite direction.

If the robot chases Daphne, turn to page 73.
If the robot follows Dorothy, turn to page 93.

THWUUUMP! Shaggy lands in an empty roller-coaster car. He looks around and realizes that he's at the exit ramp at the end of the ride. He sighs with relief.

"Whew! That was close!" Shaggy says. "I usually end up at the top of the ride."

But Shaggy's relief is short-lived. Just then an alarm sounds, and the ride starts up again. The car moves along the tracks and heads toward the top of the first drop.

"Zoinks! I spoke too soon!" Shaggy shrieks.

CLAAANG! The robot clown lands in the seat behind Shaggy. It clamps its metal hands on Shaggy's shoulders.

"Like, something tells me this isn't part of the regular safety equipment," Shaggy says with a shiver.

The roller-coaster takes off on its high-speed run. It zooms up the first incline and then drops and twists around a series of corkscrew turns. Shaggy's frantic voice loops over and over itself.

"Whooooooawhoooooawhooooo!" he yells.

Scooby-Doo hears his friend's crazy call of distress. His ears perk up, his tail straightens, and his legs get as stiff as Popsicle sticks. **ZOIIING!** Scooby extends his neck and turns his head around like a periscope, looking for his friend. Finally he spots Shaggy and the robot clown on the roller-coaster.

"Scooby-Doo to the rescue!" Scooby declares, galloping toward the ride. By the time he gets to the roller-coaster, Shaggy's dad is already there.

"I followed the footprints here," Mr. Rogers explains. He looks up at the speeding roller-coaster car. "Why is my son with that criminal clown? Is he an accomplice?"

"Raggy's in rouble!" Scooby exclaims.

"Then it's up to us to save him and catch the bad guy!" Mr. Rogers declares.

"Reah!" Scooby agrees. "Uh, how?"

"We use our brains!" Mr. Rogers says.

"Ruh-roh." Scooby gulps.

Turn to page 38.

"Who knew a simple family reunion at the circus could turn into such an adventure?" Madelyn says as she helps Velma look for her missing glasses.

"This happens to me and Mystery Inc. all the time," Velma replies with a shrug.

"You deal with clowns that turn into robots all the time?" Madelyn asks.

"Well, that's a new one," Velma admits.

"That's too bad, because we could use a little experience with that sort of thing right about now!" Madelyn says as a clanking, clown-faced creature stomps toward them.

Velma can't see more than a blur, but it's a very menacing blur. Long tentacle-like arms wave in the air. A head the size of a bowling ball bounces on a giant metal spring like a jack-in-the-box.

Velma can't see if the blur has a face. She doesn't really want to. "Jinkies!" she gulps. "Run!"

The sisters flee. Madelyn takes Velma by the hand, and the two dash down the empty midway.

Everyone else has run away, making the girls easy targets for the robot. Its long, metallic arms reach out to grab them.

The girls jump high into the air in alarm. Their legs spin like airplane propellers, and they take off! *ZOOOOOM!* They don't get far.

SMAAASH! They crash through the side of the house of horrors. *KEEEERASH!* The robot follows. Velma and Madelyn run down a dark corridor.

"It's pitch black in here. I can't see where we're going," Madelyn says.

"Good. That means the robot can't see, either," Velma replies.

Suddenly a bright beam of light shines on the girls.

"Unless it has a spotlight!" Madelyn hollers.

"Split up! It can't follow both of us at once!" Velma shouts.

"No!" Madelyn says. "I'm not going to leave you."

Turn to page 42.

Skippy-Doo runs back to the clue — tire marks.

"These weren't made by normal tires," Skippy realizes. "They're too small and narrow for a regular vehicle."

Skippy remembers something he saw in the big top. "The robot that kidnapped Mr. Blake deployed a set of wheels!"

"And this is its trail!" a voice declares.

Skippy jumps in surprise and lands in the arms of a girl wearing glasses.

"Velma!" Skippy yips happily. He gives his friend a big hug.

"Skippy-Doo, I knew *you'd* find a clue!" Velma says with a grin. "And it looks like we're both following the same one."

"The robot's wheel marks," Skippy says.

"Exactly. See how deep they are? It was carrying a heavy weight," Velma points out.

"It was carrying Mr. Blake!" Skippy concludes.

"You're good!" Velma praises. "I followed the tracks from the big top. From where we're standing, the trail leads in that direction."

"Let's solve this mystery!" Skippy proclaims.

Velma and Skippy follow the tire tracks all the way to the carnival fun house. A big sign on the door says *Closed for Repairs*.

"This would make a perfect hideout for a criminal robot clown," Velma says. "I think we should investigate."

Skippy follows Velma inside. They can't see much. The lights don't work, and everything is dark and shadowy. Strange sounds echo from deeper inside the building.

Skippy shivers. "I don't know why this is called a *fun* house," he says. "It's spooky!"

"Maybe this will help," Velma says as she switches on a flashlight. Suddenly they can see — and a frightful face stares back at them!

"Yaaaa!" Skippy and Velma yell.

"Bwahahaha!" the thing laughs back at them.

Turn to page 45.

"Scooby-Doo! Am I glad to see you!" Fred shouts as he runs up to Scooby and Mr. Rogers. The rest of the Mystery Inc. gang is close behind.

"Hi, Mr. Rogers! Where's Shaggy?" Daphne asks.

Shaggy's dad points up to the speeding ride as they all hear a voice shriek: *"Yaaaaahahaheeeee!"* A moment later, the scream is drowned out by the sound of wheels squealing against rails.

"Shaggy found the clown! Way to go, Shaggy!" Velma exclaims.

"Come to think of it, he did," Mr. Rogers says. "It's not exactly regulation police procedure, but my boy cornered the perp. Way to go, Norville!"

"Let's catch that clown and solve this mystery," Fred says. "I have a plan!"

Following Fred's lead, the gang stretches some tent canvas across the roller-coaster tracks. Then they spread a trapeze catch net behind the canvas.

"The canvas will slow the ride down," Fred explains, "then the net will catch Shaggy — and the robot!"

"I hope it works, Fred, because here they come!" Daphne says.

SQUEEEEE! ZWOOOOM! The roller-coaster car banks around the last corner of the ride. Shaggy sees what's ahead and crosses his arms over his face. He closes his eyes.

"Scooby-Dooooo!" Shaggy wails.

The roller-coaster car rips through the tent canvas like the canvas is made of wet tissue paper. Then the car hits the net. The net *streeeeetches*, and then bounces back. **SPROIIING!** Shaggy, the robot, and the car are launched into the air like a stone from a slingshot!

"Uh-oh," Fred gulps.

"Freddie! They're heading back to the big top!" Daphne shouts.

The gang runs after their flying friend. When they get back to the big top, they see an astonishing sight. An elephant sits on top of the rogue robot clown. Shaggy stands next to the elephant.

Turn the page.

"Hey, guys!" Shaggy says. "Like, say hi to Snuggles. She's one of our biggest fans!"

"Norv — er — Shaggy! You captured the criminal!" Mr. Rogers says proudly.

Just then Bo Badumdum enters the tent. "I can't thank you enough!" the circus owner says.

"Let's see who this robot really is," Velma declares. She removes the bad guy's metal head.

"Cousin Babette?!" the circus owner exclaims. "But why?"

"I wanted to help run the circus, but you didn't take me seriously!" Babette says angrily. "Robot clowns would have taken the show into the future!"

"Like, too bad they didn't work," Shaggy observes.

"I would have worked out the flaws," Babette growls. "And my plan would have worked, too, except for you meddling kids and your dog! Now, will someone tell Snuggles to get off me?"

THE END

To follow another path, turn to page 11.

The robot lumbers toward Velma and Madelyn. But as it gets closer, its spotlight reveals a service door in the wall of the corridor.

"This way!" Madelyn says. She grabs Velma and runs through, slamming the door behind them.

The robot tries to open the door, but its claws slide off the round knob. It smashes the door and steps through it just as the girls pop out of another service door nearby.

"Jinkies! We didn't get very far," Velma gasps.

The robot clown hears her and turns around. The girls dash back through the door they just came in. This time the robot doesn't even try to work the doorknob. It simply breaks down the door with its claws. *SMASH!*

Velma and Madelyn duck behind a box. As the robotic menace searches for them, they quietly try to sneak away.

CLUNK! Velma accidentally kicks something in the dark. The robot clown swivels its head around on its neck and shines the spotlight on the girls.

"That thing sure has good hearing," Madelyn comments.

The spotlight illuminates the corridor. Velma sees the blurry outline of what she kicked — a wrench. She picks it up and throws it at the robot clown. The wrench smashes the robot's spotlight.

"Great aim, Velma!" Madelyn cheers.

"I wasn't aiming," Velma admits. "Now run!"

The girls start to flee, but the robot's long, flexible arm whips out toward them. The claw snags Velma by her sweater. She struggles as it lifts her off her feet, but escape is impossible.

"Let her go!" Madelyn shouts. She tries to whack the robot's arm. But without the spotlight, she can't see where she's swinging.

Suddenly a hatch opens in the main body of the robot. A TV monitor pops out. At first there is only bright static on the screen. Then the shape of a human head and shoulders starts to take form.

Turn the page.

"Finally, I get to see who's really behind this," Velma realizes. "Except — I can't see anything without my glasses!"

The robot's other arm extends toward Velma. Her glasses are in its claw.

"I've been trying to give these back to you, but you kept running away," a familiar voice says.

Velma recognizes it immediately. "Gibby Norton!" She grabs her glasses and puts them on.

"Who is this guy?" Madelyn asks.

"Gibby has had a crush on me since we were kids," Velma replies.

"Hi, Velma!" Gibby grins and waves on the monitor. "How do you like my invention?"

"I don't," Velma replies. "It collapsed the big top!"

"I'm still working out the flaws." On the monitor, Gibby shrugs. "I just wanted to impress you."

"You try this all the time, Gibby. It never works," Velma sighs. "For a smart guy you never learn."

THE END

To follow another path, turn to page 11.

Velma and Skippy run race down the dark corridor and don't look back. **SPROING!** A giant spider drops down from the ceiling. Its long legs reach out to grab the two sleuths.

"Yipes!" Skippy yelps.

"This way!" Velma shouts. She drags Skippy down another corridor. But it's a dead end.

"We're doomed," Skippy moans.

CLICK! CLICK! CLAAANK! They hear the sounds of gears turning.

"Uh-oh," Velma gulps.

A trap door opens up beneath their feet. Velma holds tight to Skippy as her feet spin in empty air. Then gravity takes over. **THUD!** Skippy and Velma hit something plastic. Then they start to slide.

The pair swirl down a twisting chute that makes them dizzy. They zip through thick spider webs and past rows of grinning, cackling skulls. As if that isn't enough, the flashlight beam reveals that they are heading straight toward another dead end.

Turn the page.

SWOOOSH! The wall becomes a doorway just before Velma and Skippy hit it. They tumble out of the chute and land in an underground storehouse. The large space contains a jumble of circus costumes and boxes of props.

Velma shines the flashlight around the room. The light illuminates a large, ghostlike shape.

"*Mrrrfff! Arrrr!*" it moans.

Velma almost drops the flashlight in fright. She realizes the shape is a dusty sheet.

"*Errr eee oww!*" the sheet says.

"There's someone under the sheet," Velma says. She pulls away the cloth to reveal a man tied to a chair with a gag over his mouth.

"Mr. Blake!" Velma and Skippy exclaim.

Before they can rescue Daphne's dad, the robot clown returns. Thinking fast, Velma takes off her glasses and shines the powerful flashlight beam through one of the lenses. The glasses focus the beam into a laser. The robot rolls back and forth as it tries to shield its sensors.

"Help me out, Skippy! I can't see anything without my glasses!" Velma tells the pup.

Skippy reaches into one of the old prop boxes and pulls out a trick banana peel. He throws it under the robot clown's wheels.

SKIIIIID! The mechanical menace loses its balance and crashes to the floor. Velma and Skippy quickly untie Mr. Blake and use the ropes to secure the robot.

"Let's find out who's behind this," Velma declares and pulls off the robot's head.

"Dudley Doowrong?!" Mr. Blake exclaims as he catches sight of the culprit's face. "He's a business rival," he explains.

"I wanted to buy this circus too," Doowrong says, scowling at them. "I used the robot disguise to frighten people away to get a lower price."

"And you would have gotten away with it, too, if not for these kids," Mr. Blake says proudly.

THE END

To follow another path, turn to page 11.

SPLOOOOSH! SPLAAASH! Shaggy lands in a giant fish tank exhibit. His cheeks puff out as he holds his breath and tries to swim to the surface. He's almost to the top when a dark shadow blocks the sun. Giant octopus eyeballs stare back at him. Eight huge tentacles spread out like undersea vines.

"BLUUUURP!" Shaggy exclaims. He exhales and his breath turns into bubbles. They tickle the tame sea creature.

"Heehee!" the octopus giggles.

Shaggy tries to swim around the octopus, but by now he's dizzy from the lack of oxygen. Soon he can't tell if he's swimming up or down.

BONK! Shaggy bumps into something. He uses his hands to feel around. Whatever it is, it's smooth and pointed at the end. He keeps feeling.

POINK! Whatever it is, it's sharp! *CHOMP!* Whatever it is, it tries to *eat* him!

Shaggy's eyes open up wide, and he realizes he's nose to snout with a shark! Its sharp white teeth smile at him. Shaggy has no more breath but he still tries to scream.

"*BLUUUURBLE!*" Shaggy makes more bubbles.

"Heeee heeee!" the shark giggles. The octopus uses a tentacle to slap a high five on the shark's fin as if to say, *This human is fun!*

The two marine creatures lift Shaggy to the surface of the tank. Shaggy hangs over the side and tries to catch his breath. A crowd of spectators cheers and applauds. They think it's all a part of an act.

Shaggy crawls out of the tank and tries to stand, but his knees are shaking from his fright. Finally he stands up straight — and then is knocked down flat! From the ground, he sees Scooby-Doo and Mr. Rogers running away. Then the rogue robot chasing them steps on Shaggy. *SPLAAAAT!*

Turn the page.

Shaggy pulls his face out of the wet grass and looks around, trying to see what's going on. But everything has gone dark.

"Like, wait a minute! Who turned out the lights?" Shaggy wonders aloud. He hears people yelling all around him and knows one thing for sure: "Uh-oh. This can't be good."

Shaggy stretches out his arms to try and feel where he's going. He walks around like a zombie.

"Eeeek! It's a monster! Run!" someone yells.

"A monster? Where?" Shaggy shrieks and jumps in fright. He still can't see anything. Then he hears his best friend's voice.

"Rat's no ronster, rat's my pal, Raggy!" Scooby declares.

"Oh, no! Like, *I'm* the monster?" Shaggy realizes. "What a cruel twist of fate! I'm afraid of ghosts and ghouls, and now I've become my own worst fear!"

Turn to page 58.

Fred whips around in a circle but can't see who spoke to him. "Oh, no! I'm hearing things!" he exclaims. "But, if I'm *not* hearing things, then someone is actually talking to me. The only conclusion is that they're invisible! This is great!"

Just then a man steps out of the shadows.

"Oh, hi, Uncle Eddie!" Fred greets him enthusiastically. "I think there's an invisible man hiding out in this circus! That would be a great story for your newspaper."

"There's a story here, but it's not about an invisible man," Eddie replies.

"But, who — or what — was talking to me?" Fred wonders.

"Oh, that was me. Sorry to be so mysterious," Eddie says.

Fred shrugs. "So what's the story?"

"The story is about those robot clowns!" Eddie exclaims. "Who built them? Why?"

"You're forgetting one more important question," Fred observes. "Where did they go?"

"Let's start looking," Eddie suggests. "A good reporter will find a lead and follow it."

"That works for a mystery solver too," Fred replies.

The pair searches the area around the big top for a sign of the mechanical clowns.

"The ground is so trampled that I can't see if the robots left any footprints," Fred says, sighing.

"There might not be any footprints, but the robots did leave a trail," Eddie says. He points to a ribbon of dark liquid on the ground. "That's oil. One of them has a leak."

Fred and Eddie follow the trail to a large shed. When they open the door, Fred is amazed at what's inside.

"Whoa! This is incredible! Look at all this high-tech equipment," he says.

"This isn't normal for a circus," Eddie observes.

"Look! There's one of the robots!" Fred says. He points at a clown standing still in a corner.

Turn the page.

Fred walks closer. "I think it's deactivated," he says. He taps his knuckle on the robot clown's painted face. The clown's eyes snap open and glow an angry red.

"Or not!" Eddie yells.

Mechanical arms reach out to grab Fred. He jumps backward and slams into Eddie. They both fall down and watch helplessly as the robot steps toward them. **CREEEEAK! CREEEEAK!** The metal legs can barely move.

"It sounds like this guy needs some oil. It must be the one that was leaking," Fred realizes.

"That's making it slow. This is our chance to get out of here!" Eddie says.

Fred and Eddie jump to their feet and flee from the shuffling robot. But they don't get far before their escape is blocked by another robot.

"Uh-oh," Fred gulps.

"We're doomed!" Eddie says.

Turn to page 62.

Delilah and Karl march toward the midway. They can hear people shrieking. At first they think it's just families having fun on the rides. But then the screams get closer. A terrified mob is stampeding toward them!

Delilah and Karl leap out of the way just in time. They jump into a food tent. **OOF!** They land on top of Shaggy and Scooby-Doo, who are busy stuffing their mouths with foot-long hot dogs.

"What are you two doing here?" Delilah demands.

"Like, we always eat when we're scared," Shaggy replies as his whole body shakes.

"Reah," Scooby agrees as he shoves a stack of hamburgers into his mouth.

"From what I hear, that's pretty much all the time," Karl mentions.

"Which one? Being scared or being hungry?" Delilah asks.

"Take your pick," Shaggy replies as he gobbles a prize-winning pie whole.

Turn the page.

"What are you really doing here?" Delilah asks.

"Same as you — hiding," Shaggy replies.

"Marine Corps officers do not hide," Delilah snaps. "We were getting out of the way of that frightened mob."

"What could have scared them?" Karl wonders.

"Let's find out," Delilah decides. "Everyone . . . fall in!"

"Like, y-you want to actually go l-looking for whatever scared all those people?" Shaggy stammers.

Delilah nods sharply. "The first phase of any strategy is to identify the enemy," she replies.

"Rat rounds dangerous," Scooby whimpers. He pops a pile of corn dogs into his mouth, pulling out the sticks, and then swallowing.

"Like, yeah," Shaggy agrees. "Uh, we'll stay here and guard the fort."

Delilah leans down and gets nose to nose with the pals. Her eyes narrow to laser-like focus.

"I will not have my orders questioned. When I say fall in, you will fall in," she growls.

Shaggy and Scooby jump to their feet. They stand next to Karl with their backs as straight as ramrods. Scooby snaps a salute. Karl looks at Shaggy and Scooby, then moves in front of them.

"Get back into position," Delilah commands.

"But I should be in front of them," Karl protests. "I joined first, and they're new recruits."

"No dissention in the ranks!" Delilah barks. "Now, forward, march!"

Delilah turns on her heel and leads her army of three out of the food tent. They follow her down a trail of trampled grass and toppled tents. There is smashed food all over the place. Shaggy and Scooby wipe tears from their eyes at the sight of the devastation.

"What a terrible waste of all that carnival cuisine," Shaggy sniffs.

Suddenly Delilah halts in her tracks and gasps. "I don't believe it!" she declares.

Turn to page 65.

Shaggy falls to his knees and holds his head in his hands. "I promise to use my monster powers for good!" he declares as tears gush from his eyes.

PLOP! PLOP! Suddenly two big blobs of muddy grass fall from Shaggy's face. His tears have loosened the dirt. He can see again!

Shaggy looks down and realizes that he isn't a monster after all — he's just covered in mud! He starts to jump for joy when he sees a robot clown.

"Zoinks!" Shaggy gulps.

Shaggy starts to flee, but the robot extends a metal hand and grabs him by the shirt. Shaggy's legs pinwheel as he runs in place, throwing off the mud clinging to his limbs. It covers the bad robot's face. Now the mechanical monster is the one who can't see. But it still doesn't let go of Shaggy.

"I'm doomed!" Shaggy moans.

"Scooby-Dooby Doooooo!" Scooby declares as he soars through the air while clinging to the neck of the octopus.

"That's something you don't see every day!" Shaggy exclaims.

Scooby and the octopus land on top of the robot clown. The octopus wraps a tentacle around Shaggy and pulls him from the robot's grip. Scooby gives Shaggy a paw and the pair huddle together on top of the octopus.

"Thanks, pal," Shaggy says.

"Son! Are you all right?" Shaggy's dad shouts from below.

"Sure, thanks to our new friend here!" Shaggy replies. He pats the octopus on the head.

"Well, then get down here and let's close this case!" Mr. Rogers says.

The octopus stretches out one of its tentacles, and Shaggy and Scooby slide down it. The other tentacles wrap around the robot clown and hold it until the rest of Mystery Inc. arrives with the police.

"You meddling kids! You've wrecked my perfect plan!" the robot says with a human voice.

Turn the page.

"Rat's no robot," Scooby realizes.

"Somebody's inside!" Shaggy declares. "Let's take off that helmet and see who's behind all this."

The octopus uses its free tentacle to unscrew the head of the robot clown. The face of a man scowls at them.

"Bart Snarx!" Shaggy's dad exclaims. "I thought you were still in prison."

"You know this guy?" Shaggy asks.

"I arrested him back when I was a cop," Mr. Rogers replies.

"I wanted revenge," Bart admits. "That's why I stole the Scooby Snacks and tried to scare your kid. And I would have gotten away with it if not for that dog and the octopus!"

"Hey, we make a good team!" Shaggy says as he, Scooby, and the octopus slap a high-five.

"Scooby-Dooby Doooo!" Scooby agrees.

THE END

To follow another path, turn to page 11.

Fred and Eddie are trapped. There's a menacing robot in front of them and a clanking robot behind.

"Don't worry, I've got a plan," Fred assures his uncle. He grabs a pair of cordless screwdrivers and holds them up like a gunfighter from the Old West. *WHRRR! WHRRR!*

Moving fast, Fred unfastens the screws in the main body of the slow, leaky robot. All of its wiring is exposed. Fred reaches in and starts to rearrange the wires.

"Whatever you're doing, hurry!" Eddie warns as the second robot stomps toward them.

Fred yanks out two long wires and splices them together. *ZZZZZRRRT! ZZAAAAT!* The leaky robot erupts with sparks. Then it starts to spin around on its creaky legs. The robot's arms and body whirl like fan blades.

"Duck!" Fred warns.

Eddie drops to the ground. The second robot does not recognize Fred's command and walks straight into the hazard.

THUNK! THUNK! THUNK! The arms of the first robot smash the body of the second robot. Both mechanical clowns blow out sparks and come to a halt, swaying unsteadily on their feet.

"Wait for it . . ." Fred says.

WHUMP! CRAAAASH! The robots collapse on top of each other. They do not get up.

"Now, let's see who's really behind this mystery," Fred declares as he tugs at the head of one of the mechanical clowns. It does not come off. "Huh! That's weird. It's usually a mask."

"Fred! This story is about more than robot clowns!" Eddie exclaims. "Look at the writing on this high-tech equipment!"

Fred squints at the markings on the machinery. "What is that? Is it alien?" he wonders.

"No! It's —" Eddie starts to say.

Eddie's explanation is interrupted by an onslaught of federal agents bursting into the shed. Fred and Eddie find themselves surrounded.

"We're the good guys!" Fred yelps.

Turn the page.

"We know. And a grateful nation thanks you," says a woman wearing a Marine Corps officer uniform.

"Delilah Blake?!" Fred gasps.

"Affirmative. We've been tracking these foreign tech spies for a long time, but couldn't catch them with any stolen equipment," Delilah says. "Not until your mystery-solving meddling led us to them, Fred."

The tactical team wraps up the robot clowns and leaves the shed. Trucks roll up to remove the high-tech equipment.

"You didn't see any of this," Delilah tells Fred and Eddie as she drives away with the secret squadron.

"This could be the story of the century, and I can't print it," Eddie whines. "Even if I did, who would believe me?"

"Tell me about it," Fred sighs. "That's the story of my life — and Mystery Inc.!"

THE END

To follow another path, turn to page II.

Shaggy and Scooby are alarmed by Delilah's unexpected behavior. They look around, trying to see what has the Marine Corps officer so surprised.

"Wh-what is it?" Shaggy stammers.

"It's the Extreeminator . . ." Delilah replies, pointing to a massive carnival ride. "It's the planet's only combination pendulum, simulator, and launcher ride. Triple motion, audio-visual, zero-gravity — this has it all."

"It's beautiful . . ." Shaggy sighs.

"I can't believe you guys are drooling over a silly carnival ride," Karl observes.

"Calling the Extreeminator a simple carnival ride is like calling a Formula One race car a little red wagon," Delilah scoffs at Karl. She starts to run toward the ride. "Come on! Let's get on it!"

"But . . ." Karl protests.

"The Exreeminator will make a Marine out of you," Delilah declares. "Unless you're *afraid*."

"I'm not afraid of a carnival ride. But I *am* afraid of *that*!" Karl says, pointing.

Turn the page.

Delilah, Shaggy, and Scooby look where Karl is pointing. The robot is zooming toward them! Its flexible arms and grappling hook hands are extended.

"Split up! It can't chase all of us at once!" Delilah orders.

Shaggy and Scooby flee toward the Extreeminator ride. Unfortunately, the robot picks them to follow.

"It's after us, Scoob! We've got to find a place to hide!" Shaggy shouts.

"Reah! Ride!" Scooby agrees.

"That's a brilliant idea, pal! The ride!" Shaggy exclaims.

The friends sprint for the Extreeminator as the robot clown closes in on them. Shaggy and Scooby reach the ride just ahead of the robot and rush inside one of the pods.

"How do you shut the door?" Shaggy wonders as he scrambles for a mechanism. He finds it too late. The robot is inside the pod with them! The door closes, and the ride starts to move.

"Ruh-roh," Scooby gulps.

The pendulum starts to swing. The simulator projects loud noises and bright pictures. The pod reaches the top of its arc. Zero gravity lifts the occupants off their feet.

Shaggy and Scooby laugh and scream with the ride, but the robot's circuits can't handle it. When the ride is over, the robot lies on the floor in a puddle of oil, its circuits overloaded.

"Oooohhhh!" a voice moans from inside.

"That's no robot," Shaggy realizes. He pulls on the clown's hair, and a mask pops off. A queasy-looking man stares up at them.

"Who are you?" Shaggy asks.

"I used to work at the circus. I wanted revenge on Mr. Badumdum for firing me," the man confesses. "My disguise was supposed to scare people away, and he'd go broke."

"Well, you didn't get away with it," Shaggy declares. "Thanks to the Extreeminator."

"Ret's go again!" Scooby says.

THE END

To follow another path, turn to page 11.

Scooby decides to go where the helpful man is pointing. "Come on, ret's find Raggy!" he says.

He jumps up with new determination and gives the man a high-five. His paw smacks something sticky. When he pulls away, something that looks like dark maple syrup covers his foot.

Scooby tries to sniff it, but his nose is too congested. He takes a lick, but it tastes terrible.

"Yuuuuck!" Scooby gags.

"Lead the way, um . . . what's your name?" Gaggy says.

"Charlie. Charlie Equis," the man replies.

"Pleased to meet you, Charlie! My name is Gaggy. Gaggy Rogers. This is Scooby-Doo and Whoopsy-Doo," Gaggy introduces his friends.

"Hello," Charlie says, waving weakly at the canine cousins.

"Now that we know who's who, let's find my nephew," Gaggy says.

"I think I saw him heading for the big top," Charlie says.

They dash off through the crowded midway. They get halfway down the main avenue when Charlie suddenly screeches to a halt.

"Wait! There he goes!" Charlie shouts and points off to the left.

"Where?" Gaggy asks. He turns around in a circle trying to spot Shaggy.

"There!" Charlie insists. He starts to run in another direction.

The searchers follow Charlie. They race past the crowded carnival rides. They see laughing kids and their happy families. But there is no sign of Shaggy.

"Are you sure you saw my nephew?" Gaggy asks Charlie.

"Are you calling me a liar?" Charlie snaps at Gaggy. "Forget it! I'm not helping you any more!"

Charlie stomps off in a huff. No one sees him smile as he leaves.

"Fools!" Charlie mutters.

Turn to page 75.

COTTON CANDY

"Put on the brakes, guys!" Fred yells to his friends.

"Like, we're giving it all we've got!" Shaggy yells back as the rest of Mystery Inc. gets dragged along the ground.

The balloon pulls them through game tents and food stands. Even though Scooby never lets go of the mooring rope, he still manages to wrap his paws around heaps of hot dogs and cotton candy. Shaggy hangs onto the rope with his hands and opens his mouth like a bulldozer. **SCAAAARF!** He scoops up a mega-load of popcorn, pretzels, and pizza. Daphne comes out of the game tents covered in stuffed toys and bobble headbands.

"Hey, that's quite the fashion statement, Daphne," Shaggy chuckles.

SQUEEEEAK! Daphne crams a stuffed bear in his mouth.

"Guys! That didn't slow us down!" Velma shouts from the balloon. "We're still heading straight for the Ferris wheel!"

Turn the page.

"Ruh-roh," Scooby gulps.

"We're going to hit!" Velma warns.

"Don't worry, I have a plan!" Fred says.

"That's what worries me!" Velma replies.

Fred hits the burner button. Flames shoot up into the balloon cavity. Super-hot air starts to lift the balloon higher in the air.

"Yes! We're going to make it!" Velma cheers.

SPUT! SPUT! The burner goes out.

"Uh-oh . . . it's out of fuel," Fred says as he watches the balloon fall toward the Ferris wheel. "We're doomed!"

"Let go of the rope! Save yourselves!" Velma shouts to the rest of the gang.

"No way! We're going to save *youuuuuu!*" Shaggy says just as the balloon gets snagged in the carnival ride, pulling him along with it.

Turn to page 79.

Daphne goes flying through the air on the mini cycle. She has a bird's-eye view of the whole circus and carnival.

"Oh! Hi, guys!" Daphne calls, spotting the rest of Mystery Inc. down below.

"Daphne?" her friends gasp.

"I could use a little *hellllp!*" Daphne calls out to them before they lose sight of her.

"Daphne's in trouble!" Fred exclaims.

THUMP! THUMP! The ground shakes under their feet. The giant robot clown stomps toward Mystery Inc.

"Ruh-roh!" Scooby gulps.

"Run!" Shaggy shrieks.

Before the gang can flee, the huge clown walks right past them.

"Wait a minute. Why did it ignore us?" Velma wonders.

"Who cares?" Shaggy says. "Let's get out of here!"

Turn the page.

"No, Shaggy. It's after Daphne. We've got to stop it!" Fred declares.

"Like, I knew you were going to say that," Shaggy says.

"If that crazy clown is after Daphne, it will be simple to just follow it straight to her," Velma concludes.

"Let's go!" Fred says as he watches the giant mechanical monster pound through the carnival.

Suddenly the robot clown shrinks and disappears out of sight behind the concession tents. ". . . Or not," Fred says.

"Don't worry. We can still follow its footprints," Velma says. She points to the large depressions in the ground.

The gang runs along the clown's trail until the footprints suddenly disappear.

"This has got to be where it shrank down. But which way did it go?" Fred wonders.

"And where's Daphne?" Shaggy adds.

Turn to page 82.

"Something doesn't add up," Gaggy says. "Charlie said he saw Shaggy heading for the big top and then saw him at the rides. But how could he recognize Shaggy when I never told him what my nephew looked like?"

"Ruh-roh!" Scooby says.

"He used a classic magic trick — misdirection!" Gaggy realizes. "He led us all around the circus to keep us from finding Shaggy."

"Rut why?" Whoopsy-Doo wonders.

"Rat's a mystery re're ronna solve!" Scooby declares. He turns to his cousin. "Roopsy, Ri need your nose."

Whoopsy takes off his red clown nose and hands it to Scooby.

"Not rat nose. Your real nose," Scooby says with a sigh. He holds out his paw with the sticky syrup on it. "Smell this."

"What is that?" Gaggy asks.

"Ri don't know. Rit was on Rarlie's hand," Scooby replies.

Turn the page.

"And you think Whoopsy can follow the scent! Scooby, that's really smart!" Gaggy says.

"Ri won't fail you!" Whoopsy takes a deep breath of the unknown goo. He thinks for a minute. "Rit's motor oil!"

"Motor oil, like what a robot uses?" Gaggy realizes. "I'll bet Charlie Equis is connected to the robot clown!"

"They've got Raggy!" Scooby concludes. "Ret's get rem!"

Whoopsy puts his nose to the ground and follows the scent of motor oil. Gaggy and Scooby trail after him. Whoopsy leads them to a large barn filled with broken carnival rides.

"Scooby-Doo! Am I glad to see you!"

Scooby looks up and sees his pal tied to a Ferris wheel chair hanging from the rafters.

Suddenly the robot clown staggers foward. *CLANK! CLANK!* Its joints sound terrible. Its hands grasp at the friends.

"Yaaaa!" Scooby and Whoopsy yell in fright.

"That's no way to say hello to a fellow clown," Gaggy says. "Here, let's shake on it."

Gaggy grabs the robot's hand. **ZAAAAAP!** His joke buzzer sends a shock through the robot's circuits. It shudders and falls down.

Charlie Equis emerges from the shadows. "You wrecked my robot!" he says, kneeling over the fallen machine. "It was going to be a part of my act! I was going to be famous!"

"I think you need to work out a few kinks," Gaggy observes.

A short time later, Charlie is put into a police car. The police untie Shaggy and help him down from the rafters.

"Scoob, you solved the mystery!" Shaggy says proudly.

"Awww. Ri had help," Scooby replies and hugs Whoopsy and Gaggy.

"That's what family's for!" Gaggy says with a laugh. "Want to shake on it?"

THE END

To follow another path, turn to page 11.

Only Daphne listens and lets go of the rope. Shaggy and Scooby hang on and are dragged into the air as the Ferris wheel turns. The robot continues to climb the rope toward Fred and Velma.

Suddenly the ride stops.

"I found the brakes!" Daphne shouts from below. She waves at her friends as she stands next to the ride's controls. "Fred! Velma! Climb down the nearest emergency ladder! There's one on every spoke! Shaggy! Scooby! You too!"

Shaggy and Scooby look at each other. Sure enough, there's a ladder right next to them.

"Like, that's convenient," Shaggy says.

"Reah," Scooby agrees.

Mystery Inc. starts to climb down the Ferris wheel. But the clown can climb too! It grabs at Shaggy and Scooby.

"Zoinks! Now it's after *us*, Scoob!" Shaggy gulps.

The pals scramble down the ladder. The robot is right behind them.

Turn the page.

SPROOOOOING! Suddenly the robot extends its neck on its jack-in-the-box spring. Its head is right in front of them! It laughs crazily. "Bwahaha!"

"Yaaaa!" Shaggy and Scooby yell. They let go of the safety ladder and hug each other in fear. Then they realize that they are still high in the air.

The two shriek as gravity takes over. *THWUMP! THWUMP!* They land on top of each other.

THUUUHD! The robot clown lands next to them on its metal legs.

"Bwahaha! Bwahaha!" the robot laughs at its helpless victims.

"Stay away from my friends!" Daphne declares. She holds a giant wrench in her hands, ready to defend Shaggy and Scooby.

"Yeah!" Fred says. He drops down from the safety ladder and holds up the grappling hook.

"We won't let you hurt Shaggy and Scooby," Velma proclaims.

"None of us will," Mama-Doo growls. She is backed up by the Doos and Rogers and Blakes and Dinkleys. They surround the robot clown.

"I-I surrender!" the clown yelps. It twists a collar and lifts off its metal head. A human face is revealed.

"Who are you?" Daphne asks, still wielding the wrench.

"I'm a clown — a real one," the man in the suit confesses. The Bwaha Clowns are my rivals. I joined their group in disguise so I could ruin their reputation."

"And you almost got away with it, too, you meddling robot," Shaggy says as his eyes whirl in dizzy circles.

"Hey! We solved a mystery!" Mr. Rogers exclaims. "The whole family unmasked the perp!"

"You mean the *culprit*," Mrs. Dinkley corrects him. "My daughter says that's the accurate term."

"Aww, Mom!" Velma sighs.

THE END

To follow another path, turn to page 11.

"Look! There's the mini cycle she was on," Velma says, pointing. The tiny motorbike is hanging from a kiddie ride. Daphne is not on it.

"Scooby, we need your nose," Fred says.

"Rokay," Scooby replies. He sniffs the bike to catch Daphne's scent. He smiles. "She alrays wears rice perfume."

Scooby gallops off, and the gang runs after him. It isn't long before he leads them to a large tent. Shaggy's hands shake as he cautiously opens the flap.

"Like, what are we walking into, Scoob?" Shaggy asks, shivering.

The gang gasps at what they see inside. The tent is filled with an audience of circus performers watching a fashion show! Clowns in fancy costumes walk up and down a runway showing off their glamorous outfits. Daphne is at the head of the runway announcing the models. Her face is covered in glittering clown makeup.

"What's gong on?" Fred says.

"It's a fashion show, silly! Isn't it great?" Daphne replies. Then she leans over and whispers to the gang: "Just play along. I think this is a clue!"

A group of clowns rush toward Scooby and the gang. It takes only a few seconds for Mystery Inc. to be dressed in elaborate clown clothes and makeup. Then they find themselves up on the stage with Daphne.

Scooby-Doo skips down the runway in ballerina slippers and a sparkling tutu. He bats false eyelashes that are the size of butterfly wings.

"Ri feel pretty!" Scooby grins as he twirls.

"I've got to admit, Daphne sure knows her fashion and makeup," Shaggy agrees as he admires his shimmering cape.

One of the clown models elbows past the two pals and struts dramatically down the runway. Shaggy and Scooby fall off the stage and land on top of the Bearded Lady.

"Jeepers! I think I just solved the mystery!" Daphne exclaims suddenly.

Turn to page 85.

"That's not a clown. That's a professional model," Daphne declares. "And I know exactly who you are!"

Daphne grabs the clown and uses a cloth to remove its makeup. A familiar face is revealed.

"I knew it! Danica LeBlake!" Daphne announces.

"Like, your *cousin*, Danica — the French fashion model?" Shaggy gasps.

"I recognized her runway walk," Daphne says. "Every model has a style."

"It iz true, *mon ami*. I am *ze* culprit of *zis* case." Danica smiles. "Did you enjoy my adventure?"

"You planned all of this? You invented a robot clown?" Fred asks. Hearts float in front of his eyes.

"*Non, ze* robot was a disguise," Danica replies. "I wanted my cousin Daphne to have fun at *ze* circus."

"As long as Dad is okay, I'm happy," Daphne says.

"He *iz* eating caviar and croissants in a private tent," Danica assures her cousin.

"Suddenly I'm hungry for French food," Shaggy announces.

THE END

To follow another path, turn to page 11.

Scooby decides to accept help from the nice woman. She pats him on the head and smiles.

"I'll help you find your friend," she says. "But first I need to call in some reinforcements."

The woman whistles, and a pack of dogs comes running. They are large and small and everything in between. One wears a tutu. Another wears a cape.

"Circus dogs!" Gaggy realizes. "You're in good hands — er, paws — Scooby! They probably know every inch of this circus."

"I am the Amazing Astra, Canine Trainer Extraordinaire. Now, where was the last place you saw your friend?" the woman asks.

"The rig top," Scooby answers. "A clown stole our Rooby Racks!"

"Then let's return to the scene of the crime," Astra says.

"But, we followed a trail of snack crumbs to this spot," Gaggy points out.

"That could have been a false lead," Astra says. "My team will sniff out the perp."

"She sounds like Shaggy's dad back when he was a police officer," Gaggy whispers to Scooby.

"I heard that," Astra says. "And thanks."

"Rood hearing too," Scooby remarks.

The group is almost at the big top when Astra's canine crew starts barking.

"What's going on?" Gaggy wonders. He has an answer a second later, when the robot clown comes rushing toward them.

The clown holds Shaggy above its head. It cackles with crazy mechanical laughter. *HAHA HEHEHE HOOOOO!*

A blast of audio feedback makes the humans clap their hands to their ears. The dogs howl in pain. It's just enough of a distraction to let the robot zoom past them.

"*Scoooooby-Dooooo!*" Shaggy shouts to his pal as the robot carries him away.

Scooby doesn't need his sense of smell now. He has his sense of loyalty! Scooby gallops off after his friend.

Turn the page.

WHEEEEOOOO! WHEEEEEOOOO! The robot clown turns on a siren sound as it races through the midway.

The crowd separates to make way for what they think is an emergency vehicle. They are stunned to see a mechanical clown race past them instead — followed by a very large dog.

Shaggy tries to escape from the robot but can't find a way to get loose. He squirms in the robot's grip and kicks his legs. One of his feet accidentally snags part of a tent.

RIIIIP! The whole tent is pulled from its stakes and flaps behind Shaggy. Scooby chomps down on one end of the canvas. He is lifted off his paws and dragged along behind his pal.

"Way to go, Scoob!" Shaggy cheers.

Scooby feels pretty successful . . . until he sees what looms in front of them. They're heading toward a spinning Tilt-A-Whirl ride.

"Ruh-roh," Scooby gulps.

Turn to page 96.

Scooby, Shaggy, and Daphne hang onto the end of the mooring rope and try to stop the balloon from running into the Ferris wheel.

"It's no good! We're going to hit!" Fred yells down to his friends.

"We've got to drop some ballast," Velma says. "Daphne, Shaggy, Scooby! Let go of the rope!"

"I've never been called ballast before," Daphne grumbles. But she releases her grip on the rope. Shaggy and Scooby do the same, and the balloon starts to rise.

"Hey, that helped! We're going to make it!" Fred says as the balloon floats higher.

Still clinging to the mooring rope, the robot clown looks at the looming Ferris wheel. Even if the balloon misses the ride, the robot itself is still on a collision course.

The clown lets go of the mooring line and drops to the ground. **THUMP!** It lands right next to Shaggy and Scooby as Fred and Velma float away.

Turn the page.

The robot clown's eyes glow an angry red, and its arms extend toward the two pals. At first Shaggy and Scooby are alarmed. Then Shaggy seems to realize something.

"Like, what long arms you've got," Shaggy says. "I bet you can do some fancy juggling with them."

Shaggy tosses a ball to the robot.

"Reah," Scooby agrees. He adds a water bucket and a folding chair.

The robot can't help itself. It starts to juggle the items. Scooby adds a toolbox and a unicycle. The robot looks at them as if to say, I*s that all you've got?*

Shaggy and Scooby grin. They throw in a watermelon, a trumpet, a watering can, and a pot of flowers. The robot can handle it all!

"Ri'm impressed," Scooby admits.

"Yeah, but can it juggle all that while riding a skateboard?" Shaggy challenges as he shoves one under the clown's feet.

The robot clown doesn't drop a single item.

"What do you know, Scoob, he can," Shaggy says. Then he and Scooby give the robot a huge push. The clown zooms down the midway on the skateboard.

The pals run away in the opposite direction. **CRAAASH! DIIING! BONK!** They can hear the robot drop all the items it's been juggling, but they don't look back.

Shaggy and Scooby run into a building and slam the door behind them.

"I think we lost him," Shaggy sighs in relief.

"Rhere are re?" Scooby wonders. It's pitch black inside, and they can't see anything.

"I don't care as long as that creepy clown doesn't find us," Shaggy says, shivering. He leans up against the wall and accidentally hits a light switch.

What Scooby and Shaggy see makes them shriek.

Turn to page 99.

Dorothy drives the clown car off the roller-coaster loop toward the top of the arc. The giant robot clown grabs at the little vehicle as it approaches. At the last minute, Dorothy turns the car's steering wheel hard to avoid the grasping clamps. Her action causes the car to do a flip in midair.

"Uh-oh," Dorothy says.

The clown car lands on top of a tent. For a moment Dorothy is relived about the soft landing, but then the canvas starts to rip. The vehicle falls through the top of the tent.

BEEP! BEEP! THWUMP! The clown car is smacked from the side. Dorothy finds herself in the middle of a major bumper car competition.

"Sorry, Daphne! I didn't know that was you!" Fred laughs as he bangs into the clown car again.

"You're messing with the wrong Blake sister," Dorothy says as her competitive streak comes to the surface.

Turn the page.

Dorothy goes into demolition mode. *ZOOOOM!*
BANG! She smashes into Fred's bumper car, sending
it spinning into a couple of nearby cars. *BAAAASH!*

"As a racecar driver I've been trained how to
avoid a crash," Dorothy says. "But in this case it's
just the opposite! Whoohoo!"

"I might not be a professional driver, but the
Mystery Machine and I have performed some pretty
wild stunts," Fred replies.

Fred speeds up and drives his car around the
raised rim of the track. He works up enough
momentum to zoom into the air and jump over all
the other cars.

THWUMP! Fred lands right in front of Dorothy.
They face each other, ready for a showdown.

"Do you play pool, Fred?" Dorothy asks with a
knowing smile on her face.

"I like to swim laps," Fred replies, confused.
"Why?"

"This is why," Dorothy replies as she bumps
Fred's car at an angle.

Fred's bumper car is pushed into a nearby car and bounces off. It hits another car, then another, then another. Fred ricochets like a billiard ball all across the track. A buzzer sounds, and a scoreboard lights up. **WINNER! HIGHEST SCORE EVER!**

Dorothy climbs out of the clown car and smooths her lovely red hair. Fred sits back in the seat of his bumper car and gazes at her in awe.

SMAAAAASH! Suddenly a giant robot foot crashes through the tent and ruins the mood.

"Everybody get out of the tent!" Fred exclaims. He leaps into action, gathering small kids into his arms and guiding everyone else out of the danger zone.

Dorothy tries to help but is snatched by the robot. She struggles in its grip but can't get loose.

"Don't worry, Dorothy, I'll save you!" Fred shouts as the robot lumbers away with its captive. "I've got a plan!"

Then why is he running away? Dorothy wonders as Fred sprints in the opposite direction.

Turn to page 103.

The robot clown zooms straight toward the whirling carnival ride. It doesn't even try to stop.

Shaggy bangs his fists on the mechanical menace's head. **CLAAANG! CLAAAANG!** All he gets is sore fists.

At the last second, the robot swerves away from the spinning ride. Unfortunately, Scooby doesn't go the same direction. His forward motion sends him flying straight ahead.

Shaggy watches his pal sail through the air toward the whirling ride. Then he realizes that Scooby is still chomping down on the tent fabric.

"Let go, Scoob!" Shaggy yells.

"Ruh-uh," Scooby shakes his head and clenches his jaws even tighter.

SNAAAAAG! The tent fabric gets caught on one of the seats — and so does Scooby!

"Yaaaa!" Scooby shouts as the Tilt-A-Whirl spins him around and around.

"Yaaa!" Shaggy shouts as he and the robot are dragged after Scooby.

The tent gets wrapped around the trio like a cocoon. They look like a three-headed mummy.

Suddenly the canvas tears loose from the ride, and they soar through the air! *THUMP!* They land on top of a large tent. *BOUNCE!* The tent acts like a trampoline, and they spring toward another tent. *BOUNCE! BOUNCE! BOUNCE!* They rebound from tent to tent to tent.

"Like, I feel like I'm in a kangaroo's pouch," Shaggy moans.

"Rop this ride, I want to ret off," Scooby whimpers.

"*Blerrrrt! Braaap!*" the robot seems to agree.

The trapped trio finally loses speed and slides down the side of a tent. They hit the ground and unravel. Shaggy and Scooby sprawl out on the grass. The robot sparks and goes limp.

"Shaggy! Scooby! Are you okay?" Gaggy says as he and the others arrive on the scene.

"Wow! You two have some serious acrobatic skills," Astra observes. "You should join the circus!"

Turn the page.

"Thanks, but I think Scooby and I will stick to safer things like unmasking monsters," Shaggy replies.

"This is all my fault," Gaggy moans as he helps his nephew to stand up. "This was supposed to be a harmless prank."

"Huh?" Shaggy says.

"I was controlling the robot clown," Gaggy confesses. He holds out a remote control. "All I wanted was to have a fun adventure with my mystery-solving nephew."

"Well, we sure did have an adventure," Shaggy admits. "But part of the puzzle is still missing."

"What part?" Gaggy asks.

"Like, what happened to the Scooby Snacks?" Shaggy says. "Come on, Uncle Gaggy, there's another mystery to solve!"

"Scooby-Dooby Doooo!" Scooby declares.

THE END

To follow another path, turn to page II.

"Yaaaa!" Shaggy and Scooby yell.

"ROOOOAAAAR!" the lion replies. Shaggy and Scooby find themselves nose to nose with the king of the beasts! The bars of the cage are the only things separating them. The lion is annoyed at being woken up from its nap and swipes a paw at the pals.

Shaggy backpedals and jumps into Scooby's arms. "Zoinks!" he yelps. "Like, I am not a cat person!"

"Re neither," Scooby agrees as his whole body shakes.

The commotion wakes up the other big cats in the building. They sniff the air. The smell of dog makes them roar and pace around in their cages.

"Okay! Okay! We know when we're not welcome," Shaggy says. He and Scooby carefully creep backward toward the exit.

They reach the door and are about to escape when . . . *CRAAASSH!* The door bursts opens, and they come face to face with the robot clown.

Turn the page.

The robot is tangled in everything it was juggling. The mangled unicycle is wrapped around its neck. The watering can and flowerpot sit like a weird hat on its head. One of its feet is stuck in the bucket and makes the robot lean off balance.

"Ruh-roh," Scooby yelps.

"Run!" Shaggy hollers.

The pals run back toward the lion cage, but the robot's arms snake out and grab them. The lion takes one last swipe at Shaggy and Scooby before they are dragged out of the building.

"We're doomed!" Shaggy moans.

SNAAAAG! Suddenly a grappling hook grabs the robot. The mechanical menace drops Shaggy and Scooby as it's lifted off the ground.

"It looks like I caught a big one!" Fred shouts from the balloon.

The clown struggles but can't escape. It gives up and waits for Fred and Velma to land the balloon.

Turn to page 102.

Daphne and a crowd of real clowns are waiting for Fred and Velma when they land. They jump out of the balloon and stand over the defeated robot with the rest of Mystery Inc.

"Let's see who's behind all this," Fred declares.

"We already know who it is," one of the clowns says. "It is Roberto — my son."

A young boy peels off the robot suit. "I wanted to prove I was ready to perform with you!" he says.

"It's just a kid?" Fred exclaims.

"A pretty brilliant kid if he built this robot clown," Velma admits.

"This robot is not a part of the clown tradition!" the father says sternly. Then he hugs his son. "But I was impressed by your juggling!"

"Another mystery solved, and a family reunited," Fred says. "Now, let's get back to our own reunion."

"Scooby-Dooby Doooo!" Scooby shouts.

THE END

To follow another path, turn to page 11.

Fred runs to the parking lot and jumps into the Mystery Machine. He revs the van's engine.

"Dorothy Blake might be a world-class racecar driver, but I have some skills too," he says.

VROOOOM! Fred peels out in a cloud of dust. The sudden acceleration wakes up Shaggy and Scooby, who have been napping in the back of the van. They pop up behind Fred.

"Like, where's the emergency?" Shaggy asks as Fred drives at top speed.

"We're on a rescue mission," Fred replies.

"Rescue? That usually means there's danger involved," Shaggy gulps.

"Ranger?" Scooby says, nervously hugging Shaggy.

"Don't worry, I've got everything under control," Fred assures his friends. He spins the Mystery Machine around. The giant robot clown fills the van's window.

"Zoinks!" Shaggy yelps when he sees the menacing mechanical monster.

Turn the page.

"Buckle your seat belts," Fred warns as he pulls a lever on the dashboard.

FLIP! FLIP! A pair of wings deploy on both sides of the van. Then Fred pushes a button.

RRROAR! The Mystery Machine sprouts twin jet engines and takes off into the air! Fred pilots the the van straight at the giant clown.

"Yaaaa!" Shaggy and Scooby scream as Fred flies in circles around the robot.

"Relax, guys. Just pretend this is a carnival ride," Fred says as the robot swats at the airborne Mystery Machine.

"Most rides don't try to kill you!" Shaggy yells.

"Hang on, I've got a plan," Fred says. He drops the Mystery Machine toward the ground.

"Ruh-roh," Scooby gulps.

Fred fires a tow cable from the front bumper. The hook snags one of the robot's legs.

"I saw this move in the movies," Fred says as he flies around and around the robot's legs.

The cable wraps around the robot's long legs, causing it to lose its balance. The robot falls to the ground. As it hits the pavement, it releases Dorothy.

FWOOOOMP! Dorothy sails through the air and lands in a vat of popcorn.

Fred lands the Mystery Machine and runs to Dorothy to make sure she's okay. Shaggy and Scooby jump into the vat and start to eat. Daphne and Velma arrive a few moments later, along with Mr. Blake.

"Dad!" Daphne exclaims. "You're all right!"

"I was never in danger," Mr. Blake replies.

"Huh?" Scooby says as he pokes his head out of the popcorn vat. "Rut about re robot?"

"It was fake," Mr. Blake confesses. "My brother, Maxwell, was secretly filming a reality TV show about Mystery Inc. We needed some drama."

"And I got away with it!" Maxwell declares as he walks up and hugs the gang. "Your lives are so over-the-top! This is going to make a hit TV show!"

THE END

To follow another path, turn to page 11.

AUTHOR

Laurie S. Sutton has read comics since she was a kid. She grew up to become an editor for Marvel, DC Comics, Starblaze, and Tekno Comics. She has written Adam Strange for DC, Star Trek: Voyager for Marvel, plus Star Trek: Deep Space Nine and Witch Hunter for Malibu Comics. There are long boxes of comics in her closet where there should be clothing and shoes. Laurie has lived all over the world, and currently resides in Florida.

ILLUSTRATOR

Scott Neely has been a professional illustrator and designer for many years. Since 1999, he's been an official Scooby-Doo and Cartoon Network artist, working on such licensed properties as Dexter's Laboratory, Johnny Bravo, Courage The Cowardly Dog, Powerpuff Girls and more. He has also worked on Pokémon, Mickey Mouse Clubhouse, My Friends Tigger & Pooh, Handy Manny, Strawberry Shortcake, Bratz and many other popular characters. He lives in a suburb of Philadelphia.

GLOSSARY

allegiance (uh-LEE-junss)—loyal support for someone or something

ballast (BAL-uhst)—heavy material, such as water or sand, that is carried by a ship to make it more stable

court-martialed (KORT-MAR-shuhld)—to be put on trial in a military court

crater (KRAY-tur)—a large hole in the ground caused by something such as a bomb or meteorite

culprit (KUHL-prit)—a person who is guilty of doing something wrong or committing a crime

deserter (dih-ZUR-tur)—someone who leaves without intending to return

estate (ess-TATE)—propery owned by a single person or group

kiosk (KEE-osk)—a small structure with one or more open sides, often used as a stand for selling newspapers

menace (MEN-iss)—a threat or a danger

midway (MID-way)—the area of a circus or carnival in which games, rides, and other amusements are located

mooring (MOOR-ing)—the anchors, ropes, or cables that are used to hold a boat, ship, or hot air balloon in place

recruit (ri-KROOT)—someone who has recently joined the armed forces or any group or organization

YOU CHOOSE JOKES!

YOU CHOOSE which punch line is funniest!

What's Scooby's favorite snack at the carnival?
a. A hot dog — if the weather's warm!
b. A corn dog — when Shaggy gives him an earful!
c. Cheesy nachos — in the best queso scenario!

Why don't zombies like the carnival?
a. The clowns taste funny!
b. The tickets cost an arm and a leg!
c. They don't have the guts to ride the roller coaster!

What do clowns like to wear?
a. poly-jester
b. silly-cone
c. angora-ha-ha

Which performer no longer works at the circus?
a. The human cannonball — he got fired!
b. The trapeze artist — she was let go!
c. The stilt walker — he was downsized!

Why was Shaggy sweating so much at the carnival?
a. The heat was in tents!
b. The Mexican food vendors were closed, so he couldn't get chili.
c. The heat was way, way up because of Fair-in-height temperatures!

What did the egg say to the clown?
a. "You crack me up!"
b. "Your show was eggshell-ent!"
c. "The yoke's on you!"

Why couldn't Shaggy become a clown?
a. Clowns have big shoes to fill!
b. It's no small feet!
c. Because he never went to Har-Har-Harvard!

LOOK FOR MORE . . .

← YOU CHOOSE →

SCOOBY-DOO!

THE CHOICE IS YOURS!

THE FUN DOESN'T STOP HERE!

DISCOVER MORE AT . . .

www.CAPSTONEKIDS.com

FIND COOL WEBSITES AND MORE BOOKS LIKE THIS ONE
AT WWW.FACTHOUND.COM. JUST TYPE IN THE
BOOK ID: 9781496543332 AND YOU'RE READY TO GO!